MOTORCYCLE SONG

BY DIANE SIEBERT

ILLUSTRATED BY LEONARD JENKINS

HARPERCOLLINSPUBLISHERS

sharing roads with trucks and cars
both hands on the handlebars
there's the motorcycle guy
on his cycle
riding by

knows his shaft drives
knows his chains
got 10-40 in his veins
dressed in gloves and boots and jeans
loves to ride two-wheeled machines
helmet on and face shield down
riding
gliding
right through town

straddling the padded seat
foot pegs underneath his feet
bright red gas tank
frame of black
chrome exhaust pipes sweeping back
engine singing in his ears
one down
four up
through the gears

leaving city streets behind
heading out of town to find
roads that two-wheeled types prefer—
roads that set their spokes a-blur:

wide roads
side roads
perfect-for-a-ride roads
rough roads
tough roads
just-can't-get-enough roads

roads dead straight
and
roads that weave
small back roads you can't believe!

roads with speed signs, stops, and yields
roads past forests, farms, and fields

roads beneath the sun and sky
that take the motorcycle guy
to all the places that he likes
where other bikers ride their bikes:

bikers tall and bikers short
relishing their two-wheeled sport

bikers bearded and tatooed
bikers with an attitude

bikers young and bikers old
bikers who don't fit the mold
mothers
fathers
uncles
aunts
riding when they get the chance

preachers
teachers
ladies
gents
pulling trailers
hauling tents

solo riders
two-up, too
on motorcycles old and new:

lean bikes
clean bikes
polished-to-a-sheen bikes

sleek bikes
chic bikes
old, restored, antique bikes

touring bikes
and
three-wheeled trikes
and
sport bikes fast and flashy
bikes for go
and
bikes for show
and choppers low and splashy

neat bikes

sweet bikes

rumbling-down-the-street bikes

smashed bikes

bashed bikes

torn-up, totaled, trashed bikes

bikes that shimmy

bikes that shake

bikes that make your tailbone ache

bikes that putt

and

bikes that cruise

Suzukis

BMWs

Hondas

Harleys

stock or chopped

cycles sold and cycles swapped

hot bikes

cool bikes

enough-to-make-you-drool bikes

test bikes

best bikes

stripped-down or full-dressed bikes

Kawasakis

Yamahas

bikes that bring out oohs and ahs

Nortons

Triumphs

light and quick

electric start?

or

kick!

kick!

kick!

bikes with sidecars on the side

bikes and more bikes built to ride

and there's the motorcycle guy
on his cycle
riding by
spots a pothole
slows and swerves
leans into some gentle curves
engine running smooth as butter
uh-oh! now he hears it sputter
gas tank needs to be filled up
coffee? he could use a cup!

GAS AND FOOD: ahead one mile
he fills the tank and rests awhile
and watches other bikes pull in—
hmm . . . wonder where that Beemer's been?
and what about that Harley hog
complete with custom seat and dog?

the bikers have some lunch and chat
the Honda rider had a flat
the Snortin' Norton broke its chain
the Guzzi rider battled rain

what a hassle!
what a trial!
but still those bikers laugh and smile
they talk of trips and tires and tread—
of rides gone by
and
roads ahead

then one by one they wave good-bye
and there's the motorcycle guy
back on his cycle
heading north
first gear
second
third
and
fourth
then up to fifth, quick as a wink
RPMs and speed in sync
feeling good and feeling free
engine crooning right on key

helmet on
and
face shield down
riding
gliding
back to town

To Todd, Buzz, Bronson & Bob
—D.S.

To my brother Aldalbert, who taught me how to ride a motorcycle
—L.J.

Also by Diane Siebert

Truck Song

Train Song

Plane Song

Motorcycle Song   Text copyright © 2002 by Diane Siebert   Illustrations copyright © 2002 by Leonard Jenkins
Printed in Singapore. All rights reserved.   www.harperchildrens.com

Library of Congress Cataloging-in-Publication Data
Siebert, Diane.
Motorcycle song / by Diane Siebert / illustrated by Leonard Jenkins.
p.   cm.
Summary: Rhyming text describes motorcycles of all kinds and their riders, as well as the joy of the open road.
ISBN 0-06-028732-2 — ISBN 0-06-028733-0 (lib. bdg.)
[1. Motorcycles—Fiction.   2. Stories in rhyme.]   I. Jenkins, Leonard, ill.   II. Title.
PZ8.3.S5725 Mo   2002   99-087265
[E]—dc21

Typography by Al Cetta   1 2 3 4 5 6 7 8 9 10 ❖ First Edition